BENT IS THE BOW

Bent is the Bow

GEOFFREY TREASE

with illustrations by
Charles Keeping

NELSON

First published in the U.S.A., 1967
by Thomas Nelson & Sons
© 1965 by Geoffrey Trease

Library of Congress Catalog Card Number: 67-13923

Printed in the United States of America

Contents

I

When the Red Dragon wakes

Simon said the man was probably a spy. My sister Meg laughed. How could he be, when he was blind as well as old?

But then, Simon had never liked these bards, wandering into the castle out of nowhere, vanishing after a day or two like a whiff of mountain mist. Being a bailiff he was suspicious by nature, distrusting anyone who earned his dinner just by telling a story or singing a song. Being pure and solid English too (Meg and I are only half English, on Mother's side), Simon was doubly suspicious of anything Welsh.

Bards unsettled people at the best of times, he used to grumble, stirring them up to rebellion with outlandish tales of the ancient days

9

which would never come back, when Wales had been a free country ruled by her own princes.

And this was *not* the best of times, by any means, with our father hundreds of miles away, our little castle of Howell defenceless, and rumors that Owen Glendower had raised the standard of revolt in the north.

"Who on earth would want to attack Howell?" asked Mother. Simon could only chunter in his beard. She smiled and nodded to us over her needlework. We escaped down the twisty staircase and slipped into the hall, where the servants had packed up the trestle tables and were huddled round the minstrel, their ears pricked up like so many hounds.

He was chanting as his crooked fingers caressed the harp-strings. It was a strange shivery kind of music. I felt the short hairs rise in the nape of my neck and Meg's hand tighten on my sleeve. We both, of course, understood the Welsh verses as easily as if they had been English.

"Now wakes the Red Dragon from his mountain sleep . . ."

For so old a man the bard had a remarkably strong and vibrant voice. It seemed to lay hold of us. The maids and scullions craned forward, the grooms and the kennelman and the falconer, the few elderly men-at-arms Father had left to take care of us. . . . It was as though a spell had been cast on everyone in that hall.

There was an urgency in the verses. I got the notion that there was a message wrapped up in them. This was no mere tale of bygone days, no fairy story to brighten a dull evening in an out-of-the-way valley where nothing ever happened. There was a double meaning in every other line. I couldn't always get it, but I felt that most of the men could.

I edged forward, searching the stranger's face. "He sang like a nightingale," said Meg afterwards, "but he looked like a hawk." The firelight played on his craggy nose and cheekbone and hooded eyelids. It flashed on his fingernails as he plucked the strings, and on the twisted ring he wore.

No, I had never seen him before. He was like none of the bards who had ever visited Howell as they took their lonely way across the hills.

"Bent is the bow!" he chanted, and a low murmur ran round the fireside. I remembered that among the Welsh the bent bow is a symbol of war. In the morning I was determined to get the old man by himself and ask him what he meant. Young as I was, I was Father's only son and the heir to Howell. I had long ago learnt

that it counted for something. When I asked questions people had to be respectful and answer.

This time I was unlucky. In the morning the bard had gone and no-one could tell me much about him. In fact, although everybody had been spellbound by his singing, nobody now seemed anxious to discuss his visit.

He was gone, and with him had vanished the almost eerie atmosphere he had brought with him. In the broad daylight everything looked different. Our valley smiled in the bland sunshine. Even our Black Mountains did not live up to their name. They sprawled like tawny good-natured mastiffs under the blue silk of the sky.

Meg and I discussed the unknown bard as we rode our ponies up to the little waterfall by the five ash-trees, but we could not explain, even to each other, what had given us the powerful sense that something was on the move, something fresh was about to happen.

We had to turn at the waterfall and ride home. Meg had her tiresome embroidery to do and I had to practise my writing under Simon's

disagreeable eye.

That was the worst of being heir to Howell. I had to learn about documents and charters and accounts, with scraps of Latin and law and some notion of arithmetic so that I would not be cheated over rents and suchlike.

"In the Year of Our Lord Fourteen Hundred," I dated my parchment, writing slowly, my

14

tongue between my teeth, *"and the First Year of the Reign of Our Sovereign Lord King Henry the Fourth . . ."*

Working at dry stuff like that, one was soon taken out of the world of mysterious wandering minstrels and red dragons waking after a hundred years.

Yet when I awakened the very next morning I found that world all around us once more.

2

In the name of Glendower

"There's nothing to be frightened of, Hugh," Meg was saying as she shook me by the shoulder.

The castle was full of strangers, Welshmen, archers and spearmen, lightly armored for warfare in the hills. Meg said they had somehow got inside just before dawn. Nobody quite knew how they had managed it. Simon was livid with rage, she said, bawling about treachery, and they had locked him up until he cooled down. Otherwise there had been no violence and no unpleasantness at all. The strangers were behaving very politely.

We hurried downstairs to find Mother offering bread and ale to four gentlemen who seemed to be their leaders. The chief had a bony, hawk-like nose which I thought I recognised, though he was a sturdy, upright fellow with lively eyes, not veiled by drooping lids. But as his hand went out to accept the ale-tankard I saw the glint of a twisted ring, and when he thanked my mother I knew that there was only one man in the world with a voice like that.

"We mean no harm, madam. But we have orders to make sure that Howell does not fall into enemy hands."

"Whose orders?" Mother was always so wonderfully calm and dignified on these occasions. She spoke English, of course, and he answered her fluently, but with a Welsh lilt.

"The Prince of Wales."

"Prince Hal?"

She knew perfectly well that the man (Sir Thomas Rhys, he now called himself) didn't mean King Henry's son, but she enjoyed fencing with him.

"No, madam. Owen Glendower. Here is my commission."

He pulled out a parchment for us to see. It bore a seal, showing a fork-bearded man enthroned like a king.

So, I thought, that's Owen Glendower, the great rebel, the descendant of the ancient Welsh

princes, the man the bards sing about, the man whose very name makes old Simon choke with fury.

"Very pretty," Mother commented dryly. "Is it anything more than a game?"

"Indeed, yes! Glendower has been proclaimed by the Welsh people, the Red Dragon standard has been unfurled, it is certain that the Kings of France and Scotland will acknowledge him as the sovereign ruler of Wales."

"And the King of England? What will *he* say, Sir Thomas?"

"There is no King of England, madam. The last was Richard. If the English choose to obey his murderer, that is their business."

"I will not argue. This is a matter for men to settle. You are here and I am powerless. But you are a gentleman, Sir Thomas, and I trust you to see that no harm is done to my children or any of our people."

"Have no fear, madam. Your husband is a good Welshman and we have no quarrel with him."

All the same, I thought to myself, how lucky that Father was away! If he had been at home he would have been in a terrible fix. Either he would have had to fight Sir Thomas and his tough-looking band, or, if he put up no resistance, he would have been breaking his oath of allegiance to the King of England. That would have made him a traitor. When I remembered what happened to traitors I felt quite sick. Yes, it was wonderfully lucky that Father was not here.

As it was, Meg and I thoroughly enjoyed the next few days, and even Mother seemed quite cheerful, entertaining her uninvited guests.

Sir Thomas told us a great deal about Glendower and his sons and daughters and his beautiful home at Sycharth, where all the bards used to gather in the raftered hall to sing the ancient glories of Wales. Sycharth was burnt now, just a heap of ashes in a ravaged valley, and Glendower had taken to the hills. Sir Thomas gave us his version of how it had all come about, and Mother merely remarked that there were two sides to every story.

It seemed that Welshmen everywhere had rallied to the Red Dragon standard. They were flocking home from London and Oxford and even beyond the seas. Even so, I wondered how they could ever be enough to fight the sort of army King Henry would bring against them.

Sir Thomas laughed.

"Glendower has his ways and he is teaching the rest of us. How am I sitting here in your castle—and not a drop of blood shed? Henry likes an enemy he can see, and a level battle-field set out according to the rules of war. But we laugh at the rules. We don't lumber round on monstrous great horses, weighed down with armor—we ride ponies like yours, we get off and fight, and then, pouf! we're away again, like the mist streaming off the mountain. A volley of arrows from a thorn-bush is worth all your plumes and banners. Henry will never catch Glendower for *his* sort of battle. He'll be chasing a shadow in a storm!"

I was relieved by the way he spoke. Though he'd been sent to take possession of Howell, he could never hold our castle with his few dozen men if a big English force came against it. I guessed he would slip away as quietly as he'd come. I didn't want to see our poor home besieged and battered, with my mother and sister in the middle of it all.

Still, as things turned out, perhaps that was not the worst that could have happened.

One morning I woke and at once seemed to feel the quietness of the whole castle. The bustle and shouting of the past week were hushed. I could hear the birds again.

I pulled on tunic and hose and went on to the battlements. Sure enough, the courtyard below was empty save for my own groom gossiping with a maid.

When I raised my eyes and scanned the valley I saw why. A long cavalcade was creeping up the road, a glittering caterpillar of helmets and lance-points in the early sunshine. I made out the blue and white livery of Lord Whitney's men. There were at least a hundred of them.

Meg appeared at my elbow. Her fox-red hair was still unbound and whipped like a pennon in the wind.

"The Whitneys!" she said in a disgusted voice. "And I suppose they'll consider they have rescued us!"

3

A question of loyalty

Meg had a special reason for disliking our powerful neighbors from Herefordshire.

Lord Whitney, who himself looked like one of his own bulls, had a weed-like son, Stephen. I always teased Meg about Stephen, because he blushed whenever she looked at him. That was not often, because she loathed the sight of him, but you can't entirely avoid people whose estates march with your own.

We tidied ourselves hurriedly and went down to give Mother our moral support.

In no time we heard the trumpet, and then Simon announced "Lord Whitney!" in a triumphant tone, and they came clinking and jingling down the rush-strewn hall. Stephen copied his father, nursing his helmet in the crook of his arm, and both of them looked about equally red in the face, only with Lord Whitney it was due to self-importance and violent exercise.

"Lady Vaughan . . . Hugh, my boy . . . Margaret . . ." he greeted us in his usual condescending way.

"I am sorry," said Mother sweetly, "that my husband is not here to welcome you."

"Ah . . ." A queer, shifty look came over his face. "That's what I have to ask you. Where *is* Sir Robert?"

Mother was taken aback, as if she couldn't believe her ears. "With the army—somewhere on the Scottish border, I imagine. You know that as well as I do."

"Your pardon, madam, but I know nothing of the sort."

My own jaw dropped. That was a thumping lie and I could only pray that Lord Whitney would be forgiven it.

How could he *not* know? Father had received the King's summons to do his military service and supply the specified number of men from Howell. He had answered it months ago, along with various other local gentlemen. Lord Whitney must know all the names.

What was he up to?

"Certain things I do know," he went on, and I did not much like the tone of his voice. "It is reported that for the past week this castle has sheltered a band of Glendower's rebels."

"It has been held by them. We were helpless."

"Why helpless? Sir Robert is under oath to hold this place for the King."

"But Sir Robert is in Scotland!"

"So you keep saying, madam."

It was so offensive that before I could stop myself I took a step forward, clenching my fists. "Are you calling my mother a liar?" I shouted. It did not sound as well as it was meant to, for my voice was breaking at that time, and it went deep and shrill by turns.

"Quiet, Hugh," said Mother.

"I am doing my duty." Lord Whitney lowered at me, red and blotchy, more than ever like a bull. "Howell opened its gates to the rebels without striking a blow. Sir Robert is not here. He would not be the only Welsh knight who has vanished into the hills to join Glendower—"

"But you know he has not," said Mother,

wide-eyed and utterly puzzled. "How could he? Even if he wanted to? You cannot possibly believe it."

My own notion was that Lord Whitney could believe anything that suited him, however fantastic. His next words proved it.

"It is my duty to take precautions," he said stiffly. "I cannot spare men to garrison Howell, but if the rebels come back you must bar your gates and do the best you can. You must not give them food, shelter, fodder, arms—anything. And as a guarantee of your loyalty—"

"*Guarantee*, my lord?" Mother's tone should have withered him. Young Stephen winced, but his father was now enjoying himself too much to choose his words tactfully.

"Yes, madam. I shall take the children with me."

"Hostages?" Mother gave a little gasp.

"Shall we say 'guests'? Though Stephen is a little older he has always looked on them as friends."

Meg had gone pale as a tallow candle. Mother argued for some minutes but it was no good. Lord Whitney was quite set on our going, and

there was nothing to be done but order the
packing of some clothes and the saddling of
our ponies.

As Mother kissed Meg I heard her whisper,
"Take care of Hugh!" and even in the stress of
that moment I was puzzled and a shade offended.

Surely it was for me to take care of Meg?

True, she was more than a year older, but I wasn't a child now, to be looked after by an elder sister. It was for me, as the boy, to do any protecting that was needed.

"Don't worry," I told Mother. "Write to Father. Perhaps the King will let him come home and sort things out. It's only for a month or two."

She saw us off in the courtyard. She told Lord Whitney in plain terms that it was an outrage. He scowled down at her from his mountainous war-horse.

"I do this, madam, merely for security."

Then he raised his gauntleted hand and gave the signal, and the long blue-and-white column began to unwind through the archway and over the drawbridge.

4

Security?

To my surprise we did not wheel down the valley, towards England and the Whitney estates, but set our faces to the grey ridges louring across the west.

Stephen dropped back to ride abreast of us. "We may not go home for several days," he explained affably. "Father wants to catch a few

Welsh rebels first, and string them up as a lesson to the others."

Stephen was very attentive all that day, and it was impossible to talk privately without dropping into Welsh, which would have been ill-mannered and would have made him suspicious.

It was a wild, empty landscape through which we rode. Emptier than usual, for the rare figures we glimpsed in the distance seemed to be keeping out of the way. They might have been shepherds, they might have been rebel spies. Perhaps they were both.

31

Lord Whitney found no-one to question, let alone to hang. He consoled himself by burning three cottages and a water-mill. Why was there nobody there, he demanded? If they were not rebels, why had they all run off into the woods?

Personally I thought they had just been sensible, but I said nothing.

That night we lodged at Devauden Castle, where the Seymour family were pure English, good friends of the Whitneys, and mightily glad to welcome so strong a force of men-at-arms into their district. I could not blame them. They told us terrible stories of burnt manor-houses and beheaded soldiers. Glendower had ravaged the northern marches almost to the gates of Shrewsbury, and no-one knew when he might turn his main army southwards.

Meg and I did not know what to make of it. We were torn between our Welsh sympathies and our English. We wished we had Father to explain the rights and wrongs of it all, but we were glad that he was away so that, for the present at least, he was not compelled to take sides.

Meanwhile we had our own troubles. From

the way we were watched and guarded there was no doubt that we *were* hostages in the full sense of the word.

Alone at last in a tiny bed-chamber at the very top of the west tower, we had the chance to talk freely. "I don't see why *you're* supposed to be looking after *me*," I grumbled, Mother's words still rankling in my memory.

"I've been wondering a lot. All day," she said slowly, and then stopped as though unwilling to go on.

"Well?"

"I think I know what's worrying Mother. But . . . it seems so fantastic."

"Oh, come on," I said impatiently. "It's as bad as drawing a tooth!"

It amounted to this. If anything happened to Father his estates would come to me. And if anything happened to me they would go to Meg. That would mean that Meg, from being nobody in particular, would be heiress to quite a desirable estate, and that (as she admitted, going pink) a number of young men might be eager to marry her.

"Such as Stephen the Weed!" I muttered.

Until now, Lord Whitney had not encouraged his son to develop any ideas about Meg. But if by any strange mischance Meg should find herself an heiress, Lord Whitney's attitude might veer round completely. The Whitneys had always planned their family marriages craftily, so as to collect more and more land. Howell Castle and the Vaughan estates would make a most useful addition.

There were just two snags. Nothing *had* happened to Father, nothing *had* happened to me—so far. But with Father campaigning somewhere on the Scottish border and me being led captive through a Wales aflame with revolt, almost anything could happen. Or be made to happen, by a man with Lord Whitney's peculiar reputation.

He was taking us with him, he had told Mother, "for security". Whose security, I wondered?

As I tossed wakefully on my goosefeather mattress that night, I did not feel at all secure.

5

A plan to escape

We went on thinking about it the next day, snatching a few words together when we had the chance.

The more we thought, the less we liked it.

This whole business of being dragged round the country as hostages was clearly an excuse for something else, because Lord Whitney knew where Father really was and he had no reason whatever for connecting him with Glendower's rebellion. Still less could he doubt Mother's loyalty, for she had not a drop of Welsh blood in her veins.

Anyhow, why hadn't he sent us straight to Whitney Castle? The eastward road to England had been safe enough. Two or three men would have been sufficient escort. Why take us with him, mile after mile into the wilderness, making Meg share all the discomforts and dangers of a campaign?

Perhaps, I realised with a shiver, it was because accidents could so easily happen on such an expedition. If I were to die at Whitney Castle there would be many questions to answer, many witnesses to bribe. But on a journey like ours, in time of civil war, death was ever round the next corner and a hurried wayside burial was considered quite reasonable.

"You ought to escape—at the very first chance," Meg urged me. "You must."

"*We* must."

She shook her head. "Not if it makes it more difficult."

"I'm not going without you!"

"Hugh, be sensible! It's much easier for one to slip away than two. And for a boy by himself —it's rough country, you don't want a girl to worry about!"

"I can't leave you in danger."

"You're the only one in danger. Lord Whitney has nothing to gain by harming *me*. It's your duty to go, for Father's sake," she went on, clinching the argument. "Father's danger is less, the minute you get out of Lord Whitney's hands."

I saw what she meant. "He won't waste time plotting against Father in Scotland," I said slowly, "until he can make sure of me?"

"That's it, exactly."

I gave in then. It was still impossible to make any plan. We agreed that I would just have to take my chance when it came.

What I did afterwards would depend on circumstances. It would be silly to go home where Lord Whitney could pick me up again at will. I would try to reach my uncle's manor near Ludlow and send Mother a reassuring word from there.

Sometimes I wondered if we were just weaving a nightmare out of our imagination. What real evidence had we that Lord Whitney was intending anything of the sort? Once you get an idea like that, you can make every word and look appear full of sinister meaning. So it was with Lord Whitney. To do Stephen justice, neither of us supposed that he had any inkling of such a scheme. His father would not have trusted him enough. But Stephen certainly hung around us with his ears spread to catch anything we said.

I had a niggling worry lest he had overheard one of our conversations about escaping, and reported it to his father. Anyhow, from that time onward—call it coincidence or not—I seemed to be under even closer guard. Meg and I got despondent about my chances of getting away.

For three more days, in miserable weather, with rain-clouds dragging their skirts across the mountains, we went our muddy way from one remote castle to another, trying to pick up the cold scent of the rebel bands.

Then, during a noonday halt outside a small village, the clouds broke, in more senses than one.

It was not just that blue sky flowed suddenly overhead, stretching from one rounded hilltop to the next, or that a cascade of sunlight spilled down upon wet slate roofs and the white froth of the river surging between the boulders.

It was also that another kind of gap opened, a gap in the watchfulness which so far had every moment encircled us.

It was a good place for an escape. The village was strung along one bank, ending in the church.

Across the river the mountain rose steeply, densely clothed with bracken and silver birch. That wood would be impassable to horsemen. So would the river, too, I judged, because of the slippery rocks and cataracts, though it would be easy to scramble across on foot.

The column had halted by the church. The men had dismounted and found themselves seats along the low wall. A few terrified villagers were bringing them ale and such food as they had. Lord Whitney was interrogating the priest in his usual hectoring tone and Stephen was about some business his father had given him to do.

Nobody seemed to be taking much heed of us. I looked at Meg. She nodded. Casually, as if to stretch our legs after the morning's ride, we strolled the length of the village.

"I don't think it's any use," she whispered. "There's a man following us."

One of the archers was mooching along behind us. It might have been chance. After what I had noticed during the past few days, though, I felt pretty sure that he had his orders.

It was maddening. Once we were past the

end cottage a sprint of a hundred yards would carry me to the brink of the river. Then a few moments' breathless clambering and wading, partly under cover, would carry me into the complete concealment of the birchwoods. But an average bowman would have planted a shaft between my shoulders long before then.

Suddenly there was a rough shout behind us. We turned indignantly, but the order was not for us. Another man was calling back the archer. He grumbled something, but began to retrace his steps.

6

Into the clouds

It was almost too good to be true. I had to restrain myself from quickening my own stride, but I felt Meg's fingers on my arm. Slowly, yard by yard, we dawdled on till we were clear of the last building.

Not till then did I dare to glance back a second time. I could see the distant blue-and-white cluster of figures in front of the church, but nobody was following us.

I couldn't see what the river was like at this point. I didn't want to find myself confronted with some unexpected chasm, and have to go running along the bank in search of a crossing place.

"Listen," I told Meg, "you stop on the road. I'm going to walk slowly towards the bank. Ever so casually. Nothing suspicious, even if anyone

42

does see me. When I'm sure I can get across, I shall make a dash for it."

"Do take care, Hugh. And—good luck!"

There was no time for more talk. We'd said everything there was to be said. It was important to go quickly while this golden opportunity was still open.

I started sauntering across the grass. I could hear the river boiling away over the rocks. The wooded mountainside beyond was very close now, a shimmering tapestry of green leaves and silvery trunks. Once among those trees I should be free. I had a couple of hoarded oat-cakes wrapped up inside my tunic, I could speak Welsh and find friends anywhere . . .

Ten more steps and I reckoned it would be safe to start running.

"*Don't*, Hugh! Come back!"

Meg was screaming like a soul in torment.

I spun round in such amazement that I slipped and went sprawling on the wet turf. It was lucky I did.

Whish!

Something skimmed over my head. I heard something hit the rocks, and then the light

43

rattle of a wooden shaft bouncing and sliding down into the water.

I needed no more shouts from my sister to warn me off any further attempt to cross the river. A good marksman was hidden behind those cottages.

44

Meg came running towards me. She put an arm round my waist and kept very close until we got back to the road, as if defying the invisible archer to shoot again.

"I saw him," she panted hoarsely in my ear. "He must have been watching all the time. He had his bow drawn back, he was covering you every step you took. If you'd gone on, you'd have been done for."

This was something we hadn't imagined. It gave us all the proof we needed. Lord Whitney was searching for a plausible way to get rid of me. "Shot while escaping" would have been a fair excuse in time of civil war. He had staged it cleverly and he would be furious that Meg's sharp eye had spoilt everything. I wondered uncomfortably what he would try next.

For the present, fortunately, Lord Whitney had other things on his mind. A trumpet sounded. The men were hurriedly remounting and falling into their ranks.

Stephen rode level with us as we moved off up the valley in our usual place at the middle of the column. He looked excited, somehow exultant and scared at the same time.

"Father's choked the truth out of them!" he announced. "There's a nest of these scoundrels on the other side of the mountain. We're going to smoke them out. A man's going to show us a way right over the top, so we can drop down on them by surprise. You'll see some fun before the night's over!" And he spurred away to join his father in front.

"Self-satisfied little—" grunted Meg.

Now, as if to match our mood of gloom and disappointment, the actual clouds were rolling back. The mountain turned from gold to leaden grey. Then the top vanished completely, as swathes of dirty white mist came dragging across the slopes.

The track, if you could call it a track, followed a stream which came splashing down in pale threads like spilt milk. Soon the men-at-arms had to dismount and coax their heavy beasts. Our ponies might have managed the climb, but progress was so slow that it seemed better to get off like the others.

Looking back, I saw that we had already lost the village and the green floor of valley meadows. We were in the clouds we had seen from below.

46

They wrapped round us like sodden cloaks. Then a wind came moaning over the ridge, icy to nose and cheek, and the rain followed, hissing and vicious.

All colour went out of the view. At thirty paces the peacock blue of the Whitney livery was reduced to a shadowy drabness. The polished helmets misted over.

The slope grew less steep. That only meant it was boggy underfoot. We plodded and squelched up a trough-like hollow towards an invisible skyline. The column began to bunch up behind the leaders. I heard Lord Whitney just in front. He was cursing the storm which had chosen this moment to break upon us and accusing the guide of losing the way. A lilting voice answered him:

"If your lordship will halt here a moment, I will run forward and make sure that we have not missed the fork!"

"Hi—wait!" Lord Whitney bellowed. But Stephen said, "It's no use, Father, he's gone."

"I don't trust these fellows," said Lord Whitney, and I saw his point. As the minutes passed, and we all stood there, horses and men alike bowing their heads against the slanting rain, I felt more and more certain that the guide would never come back.

Then, suddenly, out of the racing clouds on both sides of us came the blare of trumpets and the whizz of arrows.

7

Firelight in the woods

It was the second time that day I had been shot at, and I did not like it. To be shot in mistake for one of Lord Whitney's retainers would have been bitter indeed.

"Quick!" I gasped. "Get between the ponies!" We stood like that for some moments, huddled together, using our poor beasts as shields.

There was a wild din both in front and behind. Dim shadows capered against the mist and vanished again. Trumpets blew, swords and spears clashed together, savage voices mingled in a babel of English and Welsh.

"Hugh!" said Meg. "This is our chance!"

"It looks like it—"

The battle had split into two. Just ahead of us we could hear Lord Whitney rallying one group of his men. Behind, and below us, the rear of the column seemed to be fighting its way up to join him. For a moment we stood in the gap between, and nobody was guarding us.

It was a pity we had to leave the ponies but there was no choice. We had to get off the track and strike across the boggy mountainside. Two feet were better than four. Even for us the going was bad enough. The rebels had picked a devilish place for their ambush.

The noise faded behind us. The ground grew firmer and took a downward curve. We must have crossed some sort of a crest. The rain died away and the mist began to thin. Treetops swam into view at our feet.

"We'd better get down off the skyline," I said, "before anyone sees us. Do hurry!"

"I've lost one of my shoes."

Meg looked very bedraggled, holding up her sodden skirt and limping over the coarse grass tussocks.

"Never mind," I said. "We've lost Lord Whitney as well!"

"Where are we? Which way are we going?"

"It doesn't matter, does it, for the moment?"

"I suppose not." Meg sounded a little doubtful. But then she hadn't been prepared for this.

It was easier for me. I'd been all keyed up for days to make this dash for freedom, though I hadn't bargained for quite such tough conditions—or for the responsibility of looking after Meg.

I should have been a good deal more worried if I had realised then all the horrors of the civil war that was to rage throughout the country during the next few years. That autumn evening I still had faith in the friendliness of ordinary people. In Wales no hungry stranger was ever turned from the door—and who (except a man like Lord Whitney) would harm a boy and girl?

We wandered about in that wood for hours. The sky overhead never cleared enough to give us a glint of sunset, so we had no clue to direction. It got very dark. Not a star showed, much less the moon. We split one of my precious oatcakes, but kept the other. Meg was exhausted and wanted to lie down. I was not much better myself, but I did not mean us to spend a night in the open if we could help it.

Then we saw the ruby glow of the first fire, playing on the slender white birch trunks and the lazy spirals of smoke. There were more fires . . . two, three, four . . . twinkling along the edge of the wood. A whole encampment.

"Suppose it's the Whitneys?" Meg breathed in my ear.

I pooh-poohed the notion. After that ambush

on the mountain Lord Whitney would never pitch a camp like this, a target for every Welsh-man who could bend a bow. The men round those fires must be rebels, perhaps Sir Thomas Rhys was there. . . . Even if he was not, it would be all right, provided we spoke Welsh.

We crept forward until we could see men sitting round the nearest of the fires. There was a wonderfully savory smell from mutton roasting on spits. Then, in horror, I recognised one of the faces lit up by the fire-light.

It was Stephen's.

8

The man with the forked beard

I clawed at Meg's arm. "Back!" I whispered.

But we had gone too near. Someone had seen us. As we turned, sick with fear and disappointment, we were jumped on by rough-handed shadows and hauled forward into the encampment.

Then we saw to our relief that Stephen the Weed had cord round his ankles and wrists. Scared and dismal, he looked more weedlike than usual.

"The Vaughan children? Thank God!" cried a Welsh voice we knew, and there was Sir Thomas Rhys coming towards us with outstretched arms from another of the fireside groups.

As soon as he had satisfied himself that we were quite unhurt, only footsore and ravenous,

he put his hands on our shoulders and pushed us forward to the fire he had just left.

There, with only an old tree-stump for a throne, sat the man whose face we had seen on the wax seal a week or two ago, the man with the forked beard, Owen Glendower, the newly proclaimed Prince of Wales.

Sir Thomas presented us, I bowed and Meg dropped a curtsey. Glendower smiled and said a kind word, for he was well used to young people with his great brood of sons and daughters. He told us to sit down and warm ourselves, other men thrust meat and drink into our hands, and then (thank goodness) everybody forgot about us for a while. The talk washed over our heads as though we were not there.

Some echoes of that talk were to ring in my memory for the rest of my life. Glendower's dream of an independent Wales under the Red Dragon flag, holding her own against England as an equal ally of France and Scotland . . . a royal court at Harlech Castle, a Welsh Parliament, Welsh universities . . .

It was a golden dream which those eager

voices conjured up in the camp-fire glow. I was nearly won over by it. I found myself wishing I was a few years older, so that I could help in making it come true.

"It will bring wonderful things to Wales," I murmured, but Meg whispered back, with a bitterness that surprised me, "It will bring death and destruction, more like." Women are often disbelieving when men have splendid schemes.

After a while we grew sleepy with all the talk, our tiredness, and the ale they had given us with our supper, but the mention of our own names startled us into wakefulness again.

"Sir Thomas," Glendower was saying, "you had better ride back to Howell with them tomorrow."

"Forgive me, my lord," I blurted out, "but is it safe for us to go home? Lord Whitney—"

"Lord Whitney is dead," said Glendower. "I do not think you will be troubled any more. But that reminds me: what shall we do with this son of his?"

I realised then why Stephen had been looking so utterly lost and woebegone. Meg, always the warm-hearted one, exclaimed: "Oh, let him go, my lord! Please!"

Glendower looked stern and stroked his beard. "But *he* is now Lord Whitney. *He* becomes lord of five castles, hundreds of retainers—"

"And that's the best reason for setting him free," she explained shrewdly. "They'll be far less dangerous to you, my lord, if Stephen commands them than if somebody else does. I know Stephen!"

The men roared with laughter, but Sir Thomas supported her in all seriousness and vowed she was a good judge of character.

So it was decided, and Sir Thomas went across to where poor Stephen was sitting and told him the good news. In the morning he would be set free with half a dozen of his captured men, and they could take his father's body home for honorable burial. It was made clear to him that he owed his liberty to Meg's pleading.

Sir Thomas was grinning when he came back to us. "You seem," he told her with a chuckle, "to have earned the undying gratitude and devotion of the new Lord Whitney!"

Meg made a face. "That," she said, "is the one thing which is troubling me!"

But it was a small thing, and it was forgotten by the next morning when we took leave of the Prince, mounted our own ponies once more, and set off home with our escort. The sun was shining again, the birchwood was alive with bird-song, and like the clouds on the mountain all our cares had been blown away.